THIS BOOK BELONGS TO

. . . .

This book was donated by our local community for Roxeth's Reading like a Writer Week 2019

I celebrated World Book Day 2017
with this brilliant gift from my local
bookseller and Simon & Schuster

Shout "hip-hooray for underpants!"
Let's sing this silly song,
Underpants are WONDERPANTS
We LOVE pants all day long!

Aliens love underpants,
They're fun and stretchy-snappy,
And pinging pants elastic,
Makes the aliens SO happy!

Monsters all love underpants
In every shape and style.
They look EXTREMELY silly –
But it makes the monsters smile!

Dinosaurs love underpants,
And it's no big surprise,
They love their pants DINORMOUS –
To fit their GIANT size!

Pirates SO love underpants,
In patterns bright and bold,
And love to sing and dance around
Their treasured PANTS of GOLD!

Yes! EVERYONE loves underpants.
That's why we're ALL together,
To celebrate fun underpants –
We LOVE our pants forever!

So shout "Hooray for underpants!"
YES! Underpants are fun!
In each bright colour, shape and size —
We love them — EVERY ONE!